J. Bingham is an author of a unique set of books, inspired through play with her son. Born and raised in Northern Ireland, J. Bingham is a fresh addition to the world of children's literature. J. Bingham's desires are to inspire and encourage others to connect with their children through words, songs and play, which began with her first publication *Hip Hooray and Robot Ray Go Sailing*.

HIP HOORAY AND ROBOT RAY GO SAILING

J. BINGHAM

AUSTIN MACAULEY PUBLISHERS™

LONDON • CAMBRIDGE • NEW YORK • SHARJAH

A CIP catalogue record for this title is available from the British Library.

ISBN 9781398436077 (Paperback)
ISBN 9781398436084 (ePub e-book)

www.austinmacauley.com

First Published 2023
Austin Macauley Publishers Ltd®
1 Canada Square
Canary Wharf
London
E14 5AA

Dedicated to B.D.B. My inspiration.

Thank you to the team at
AUSTIN MACAULEY PUBLISHERS
for their advice and support.

We have got a boat.
We have got a boat.

Hey ho my dearie oh,
We have got a boat.

I can see a whale.
I can see a whale.

Hey ho my dearie oh,
I can see a whale.

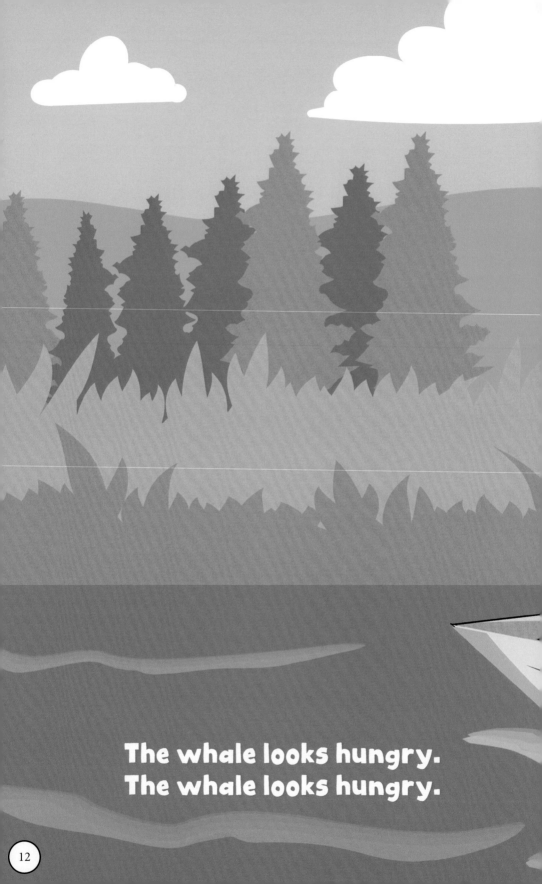

The whale looks hungry.
The whale looks hungry.

12

Hey ho my dearie oh,
The whale looks hungry.

Into the belly we go.

Into the belly we go.

Hey ho my dearie oh,
Into the belly we go.

We'll tickle him to get out.
We'll tickle him to get out.

Hey ho my dearie oh,
We'll tickle him to get out.

The whale spat us out.
The whale spat us out.

Hey ho my dearie oh,
The whale spat us out.

The whale needs our help.
The whale needs our help

Hey ho my dearie oh,
The whale needs our help.

Off to home we go.
Off to home we go.

Hey ho my dearie oh,
Off to home we go.